Ready Steady Read!

LEVEL 1

Dear Parents,

Congratulations! Your child has embarked on an exciting journey – they're learning to read! As a parent, you can be there to support and cheer them along as they take their first steps.

At school, children are taught how to decode words and arrange these building blocks of language into sentences and wonderful stories.

At home, parents play a vital part in reinforcing these new-found skills. You can help your child practise their reading by providing well-written, engaging stories, which you can enjoy together.

This series – **Ready, Steady, Read!** – offers exactly that, and more. These stories support inexperienced readers by:

- gradually introducing new vocabulary
- using repetition to consolidate learning
- gradually increasing sentence length and word count
- providing texts that boost a young reader's confidence.

As each book is completed, engaging activities encourage young readers to look back at the story, while a Picture Dictionary reinforces new vocabulary. Enjoyment is the key – and reading together can be great fun for both parent and child!

Prue Goodwin
Lecturer in Literac

1

How to use this series

The **Ready, Steady, Read!** series has 4 levels.
The facing page shows what you can expect to find
in the books at each level.

As your child's confidence grows, they can progress
to books from the higher levels. These will keep them
engaged and encourage new reading skills.

The levels are only meant as guides; together, you and
your child can pick the book that will be just right.

Here are some handy tips for helping children who are
ready for reading!

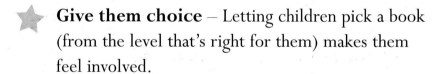

Give them choice – Letting children pick a book
(from the level that's right for them) makes them
feel involved.

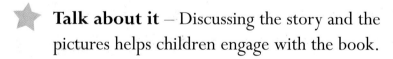

Talk about it – Discussing the story and the
pictures helps children engage with the book.

Read it again – Repetition of favourite stories
reinforces learning.

Cheer them on! – Praise and encouragement
builds a child's confidence and the belief in their
growing ability.

LEVEL 1 For first readers

* short, straightforward sentences
* basic, fun vocabulary
* simple, easy-to-follow stories of up to 100 words
* large print and easy-to-read design

LEVEL 2 For developing readers

* longer sentences
* simple vocabulary, introducing new words
* longer stories of up to 200 words
* bold design, to capture readers' interest

LEVEL 3 For more confident readers

* longer sentences with varied structure
* wider vocabulary
* high-interest stories of up to 300 words
* smaller print for experienced readers

LEVEL 4 For able readers

* longer sentences with complex structure
* rich, exciting vocabulary
* complex stories of up to 400 words
* emphasis on text more than illustrations

Once you have read the story, you will find some amazing activities at the back of the book! There are Excellent Exercises for you to complete, plus a super Picture Dictionary.

But first it is time for the story . . .

Ready?

Steady?

Let's read!

Linda Jennings   Basia Bogdanowicz

Fred

LITTLE TIGER PRESS
London

Fred had a new cat flap.
He looked through it . . .

OH!

But Horrible Harry
was <u>outside</u>!

"Can't catch me!"
said Fred.

sssss!

But Harry nearly did.

Fred hid.

Then Horrible Harry tried
to come in.

"I don't like my cat flap,"
said Fred.

Later, Fred wanted to
go outside.
  "Use your cat flap,"
said Katie.

MIAOW!

"I *hate* my flap!"
said Fred.

Katie pushed
Fred outside.

Fred hid.

"Supper!" called Katie's mum.

Fred crept back inside
through the open door.

"You must use your cat flap!"
said Katie's mum.

So Fred tried . . .

. . . very hard.

W H E E E !

CRASH!

M I A O O W !

YIPPEE!

Harry fled.
  "My cat flap is brilliant!"
said Fred.

Excellent Exercises

Have you read the story? Well done!
Now it is time for more fun!

Here are some questions about the story. Ask an adult to listen to your answers, and help if you get stuck.

Scaredy Cat

In this story, Fred is frightened of his cat flap.
Is there anything that frightens *you*?

Garden Goodies

Can you name some of the objects in this picture?
What kind of things do you have in *your* garden?

Poor Fred

Now describe what Fred is doing in this picture.

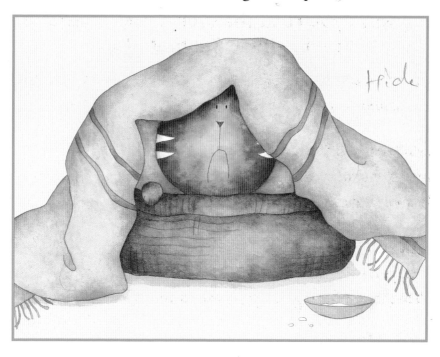

Try, Try, Try Again!

Can you remember if Fred uses his cat flap in the end?
What things have *you* learned to do?

Picture Dictionary

Can you read all of these words from the story?

brilliant

feeling brave

crept

door

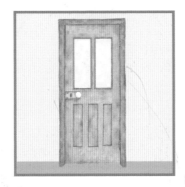

flap

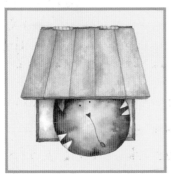

Fred

Harry

hid

Katie

pushed

supper

Can you think of any other words that describe these pictures – for example, what colours can you see? Why not try to spell some of these words? Ask an adult to help!

Can't You Sleep, Dotty?

Dotty has tried everything. But she just cannot sleep. Soon all her friends are trying to help her. But will anything work . . . ?

My Turn!

When Oscar and Tilly go to the playground, they are not keen to wait their turn. Will the two friends find a way to play together?

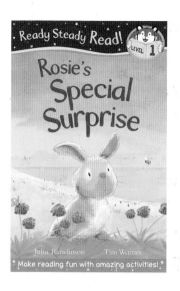

Rosie's Special Surprise

Nosy Rosie likes to know everything about everything. So when Daddy Rabbit says he has a special surprise, she hops off to look for it. Whatever could it be?

What Bear Likes Best!

Bear really likes to have fun. But all of his friends are busy and he keeps getting in the way! Will it ever be time to play?

For all the tribe — L J
Dla Babci i Dziadzia — B B

LITTLE TIGER PRESS, 1 The Coda Centre, 189 Munster Road, London SW6 6AW
First published in Great Britain 1995
This edition published 2013
Text copyright © Linda Jennings 1995, 2013
Illustrations copyright © Basia Bogdanowicz 1995, 2013
Printed in China
978-1-84895-664-3
LTP/1800/0585/0413
2 4 6 8 10 9 7 5 3 1

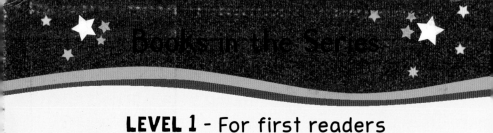